MAY 2023

The World of Emily Windsnap

The Truth About Aaron

The World of Emily Windsnap

The Truth About Aaron

Liz Kessler

illustrated by Joanie Stone

CANDLEWICK PRESS

Dedicated to all the boys out there
who want to be merpeople, too.
You can be anything you want to be!
LK

For Viktor
JS

Text copyright © 2023 by Liz Kessler
Illustrations copyright © 2023 by Joanie Stone

First edition 2023

Library of Congress Catalog Card Number 2022936942
ISBN 978-1-5362-1524-3 (hardcover)
ISBN 978-1-5362-2556-3 (paperback)

23 24 25 26 27 28 APS 10 9 8 7 6 5 4 3 2 1

Printed in Humen, Dongguan, China

This book was typeset in Stempel Schneidler.
The illustrations were created digitally.

Candlewick Press
99 Dover Street
Somerville, Massachusetts 02144

www.candlewick.com

CONTENTS

CHAPTER ONE
Visitors

Aaron was excited. His mom had told him that guests were coming for dinner! And even better, his best friends, Emily and Shona, would be visiting, too.

Aaron lived in a castle on an island in the middle of the ocean, so he didn't have many guests. Aaron had met Emily and Shona when they were exploring one day. They'd discovered the castle and the three of them had been best friends ever since.

Aaron looked out his bedroom window. Were those tails sparkling in the waves?

Yes! They were here.

Aaron ran to the pool underneath the castle.

He slipped into the water and began to swim.

As he swam, a familiar feeling spread through his legs. They stiffened up, joined together . . . and turned into a tail!

Aaron was a semi-mer like his friend Emily. That meant he was a boy on land but when he was in water he became a merboy.

Aaron flicked his tail and headed into the tunnel that led out to the ocean.

He swam to the surface and saw two heads pop up nearby.

"Emily! Shona!" he called.

They swam over.

"We passed a ship on our way here," Emily said.

"It was HUGE!" Shona added. "And it looked like it was coming to the castle."

"That must be our dinner guests," Aaron said.

"Your guests have a very fancy ship!" Emily said.

"Let's get a closer look," said Aaron.

They dived under the water, laughing and splashing and chatting.

CHAPTER TWO
The Ship

As they swam, the three friends talked about what they had been up to.

"Shona won the Shiprock School talent show with her singing!" Emily said.

"That's amazing!" Aaron said.

Shona blushed, then said, "Well, Emily swam at the beach in front of everyone!"

"They all got to see my tail. It was swishy!" Emily added.

Aaron smiled. He was glad they were happy, but he didn't have anything exciting to share. There were no other kids at the castle to have adventures with. He wished he had some news he could tell his friends, something special he had done.

Then suddenly the ship was right in front of them.

It *was* fancy . . . and huge! The hull gleamed with gold, and the mast stretched up into the clouds. A pod of dolphins swam behind it.

The three friends swam closer. They could hear voices on the deck above them.

"I think we should tell him to give up the search," they heard someone say.

"I agree. He still expects us to locate this precious thing, but we've been looking for years. We'll never find it."

"What was that about?" Emily asked after they dived back under the water.

"Maybe they're pirates!" Shona said, her eyes wide.

"Or smugglers," Aaron added.

"Or just plain thieves," Emily finished.

"Come on, let's get back to the castle," Aaron said. He wasn't excited about their dinner guests now. He was worried.

"Meet us in the pool after dinner," Emily said, "so you can tell us all about them!"

CHAPTER THREE
Dinnertime

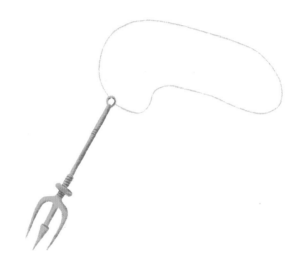

After the ship docked, the crew came ashore to the castle. They greeted Aaron's mother.

Then one of the men came over to Aaron.

"That's a nice necklace you have there," the man said to Aaron.

He was pointing to the silver chain around Aaron's neck. It had a pendant shaped like a big fork with three prongs.

"It was his father's," Aaron's mom said sadly. "He wore it every day."

"It's a very unusual pendant," the man said. "May I show it to some of my shipmates?"

"Aaron, take it off so they can have a good look at it," his mom said.

Aaron took the necklace off and gave
it to the man, who walked back to the rest
of the crew. They looked at the pendant,
speaking in low voices.

Then someone announced, "Ladies
and gentlemen, dinner is served."

Suddenly Aaron realized how hungry he was. He'd been too busy having fun with Emily and Shona to eat lunch!

When dinner was over and the crew had returned to their ship, Aaron went to meet Emily and Shona at the pool. Then he realized something terrible.

"What's wrong?" Shona asked when she saw the look on his face.

Aaron pointed at his bare neck. "One of the men asked to see my necklace at dinner, but he never gave it back!"

CHAPTER FOUR
Captured!

"We have to go get it," Emily said.

"We?" Aaron asked.

"Of course!" Shona said. "We're not going to let you face pirates on your own."

Together they swam out to the bay where the ship was anchored.

"Look," Emily said, pointing at a ladder hanging from the deck.

"I'm going up," Aaron said. "You stay here and wait for me. Go get my mom if I'm not back in ten minutes."

The girls nodded.

Aaron pulled himself up the ladder and onto the deck.

Just as his tail was starting to turn back into legs, he heard a gasp.

The man from dinner had seen his tail!

Before Aaron could get away, the man grabbed his shoulders.

"You'd better come with me," he said.

The man led Aaron down a staircase.

As they walked, Aaron could feel his heart

thudding in his chest. Where was the man taking him?

Even though he was afraid, Aaron couldn't help but notice that the inside of the ship was even more beautiful than the outside. It was stunning!

"These men must be very good pirates,"
Aaron thought. So why did they want his
necklace so much? And what were they
going to do with him now that they had
seen his tail?

The man opened a door. "Go in," he
said. Then he closed the door behind Aaron.

Aaron waited, his heart racing.

CHAPTER FIVE
Neptune

"COME!" a loud voice suddenly boomed from the other side of the room. Another door had opened that led to the sea. Outside was a chariot surrounded by dolphins.

Aaron realized right away it was King Neptune!

Aaron knew that King Neptune was a stern ruler with a bad temper. When he got angry, he could turn a calm sea into waves as big as cliffs.

And now he was holding Aaron's necklace! Aaron's heart thudded even harder.

"Here," Neptune said. "I believe this is yours."

Aaron stepped forward and took the necklace from Neptune. "Thank you, Your Majesty," he said, bowing.

"You're welcome," Neptune said. "I never intended to keep it."

"But what about the pirates?" Aaron asked.

Neptune narrowed his eyes. "Pirates?"

"I heard them talking. They said they were looking for a precious thing. And then they took my necklace and gave it to you.

And now you're giving it back to me, but
I don't understand why!"

Neptune burst out laughing.

Aaron felt his cheeks flush. "I don't see what's so funny," he said. Then he noticed Neptune's trident. It was the same shape as his pendant!

"You're right," Neptune said. "I have been looking for something

precious. And yes, I have found it. But the
precious thing isn't your necklace!" he said.
"That was just what proved that the most
precious thing was here. And then, when
I heard about your . . ." Neptune pointed
at Aaron's legs.

"My tail," Aaron said.

"Yes, your tail," Neptune said. "That was when I knew for sure."

"Knew what?"

"That my search was over. We finally found it. My long-lost descendant! I've been looking for you for many years."

Aaron gasped. "Me?"

"Yes, my boy," Neptune said. "*You* are the precious thing I've been looking for!"

CHAPTER SIX
Celebration

Just then the door burst open. Aaron's mom and Emily ran into the room.

"Aaron, are you OK?" Emily asked. Then she saw King Neptune.

"Your Majesty," she said, dropping into a curtsy.

"What's going on?" Aaron's mom
asked.

"I'm fine," Aaron said. "More than
fine."

"I will explain everything," Neptune
said. "I have been searching the oceans
for years looking for my family. My true
love—my wife—was a human. We had

children, and they had children, and so on. However, since humans and mers haven't always gotten along, I lost touch with them. But now I have found the youngest member of my family, and I will make sure I never lose you again!"

Aaron's mom hugged him and smiled. "I'm so glad you're safe," she said. "I was worried when Emily and Shona came and said you'd been taken by a man on the ship."

Neptune clapped his hands. "So now, let's celebrate!"

The crew of the ship and everyone from the castle joined them. There was music and food. Aaron, Emily, and Shona ate till their stomachs hurt.

Even the crew who had taken Aaron's pendant were smiling and laughing.

Merpeople danced in the water,
spinning so fast they made whirlpools
around the ship.

Aaron turned to his friends. "Come on," he said. "Let's celebrate our way."

"Yes, Your Majesty," Emily and Shona

said together.

Then they flicked their tails so fast
that they popped out of the water, twirled
in the air, and ended with a bow.

Aaron stared at them.

Then the girls burst out laughing.
Aaron laughed, too. Soon all three of them
were giggling so hard they couldn't stop.

Together they swam and ducked and
dived. They chased one another, splashing
and laughing and talking nonstop.

Their tails made sparkly diamonds in the waves as the moon shone on the water behind them.

And that was when Aaron realized he *was* special, after all. Not because he was related to a king.

But because he had the best friends in
the whole world.